THE MIDNIGHT GHOSTS

Emma Fischel

Illustrated by
Adrienne Kern

Series Editor: Gaby Waters

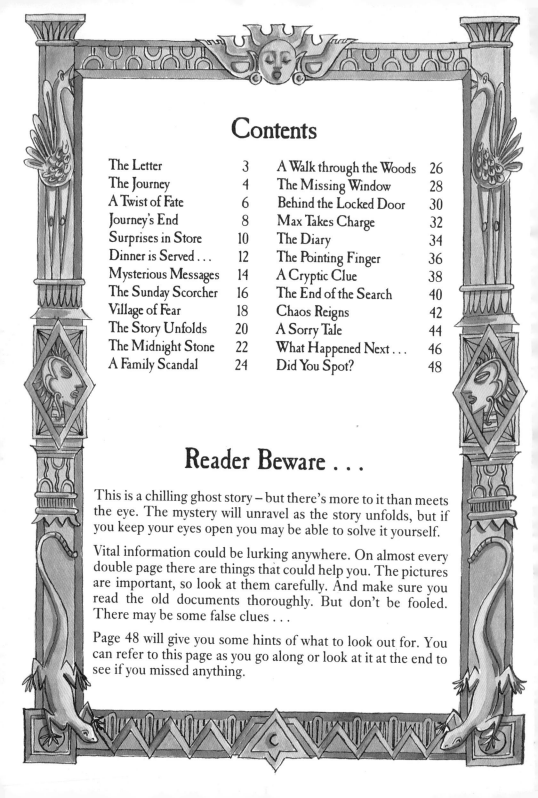

Contents

Reader Beware . . .

This is a chilling ghost story – but there's more to it than meets the eye. The mystery will unravel as the story unfolds, but if you keep your eyes open you may be able to solve it yourself.

Vital information could be lurking anywhere. On almost every double page there are things that could help you. The pictures are important, so look at them carefully. And make sure you read the old documents thoroughly. But don't be fooled. There may be some false clues . . .

Page 48 will give you some hints of what to look out for. You can refer to this page as you go along or look at it at the end to see if you missed anything.

The Letter

A nt and Sally read through the letter with some trepidation. There was no getting out of it now. They really were going to stay at Twelve Bells End. It was a pity they couldn't remember more about the house or cousin Max. But everything they had heard led them to think that this could be a very strange week.

"You never know, it might be fun," said Ant uncertainly . . .

Ant

Sally

Manley, me and darling Max

POSY 7th Nov

Outside the family villa

Twelve Bells End,
Gloomwood Road,
Middle–Knight–on–Sea.

November 6th

Dearest Sally and Anthony,

Isn't this a dreary time of year? Your uncle Manley and I simply *must* escape to Mythika for a week's sun. Thrilled you can pay our precious son Max a visit while we are away. He does so need company of his own age. How tiny you were when we last saw you! Do you remember how Max cut up your skipping rope and fed it to you, saying it was spaghetti — such high spirits!

You'll find us a full household. People visit and, somehow, never leave. We seem to have had some unfortunate accidents over the years, though. And, strangely, all at midnight too! (Dear Manley was never the same after the accident with the cheese grater seven years ago this week, and — between ourselves — the others are not much better. Then there's the professor. Hardly had he arrived (just over a couple of years ago now and without two pennies to rub together) than, overnight, he almost completely lost his hearing.)

Our fortunes seem to have taken a downward turn these last two years. I'm afraid the house is a trifle shabby. (Mrs Mopps, of course, has been an absolute treasure since she arrived in June — although one could wish for just a *shade* more enthusiasm for the dusting.) Too bad there seems to be no one to take over the title and restore the house to fortune! It's nearly fifty years now since Melrose passed away. And where is Magnus? So sad Magnolia took him away when he was so small (rumour has it that he was seen three years ago on Saddlesore racecourse, gambling away his fortune).

Well, darlings, we'll expect you on the eleventh. All love, your auntie Crystal xxx

PS I dug out a few photos for you. The one of my sister Posy was taken on the night of her tragic fall. The happy couple are your great-aunt Myrtle and great-uncle Harvey.

The Journey

A ll along the platform the last stragglers were slamming doors shut behind them. Ant and Sally leapt on to the train, gasping. The guard blew the whistle and the train pulled slowly out of the station.

Sally barged her way through the carriage in search of an empty window seat. Ant followed her, red-faced and puffing under the weight of most of their luggage. Sally settled herself comfortably in the seat facing forwards while Ant collapsed in a heap opposite her.

Sally started to feel more hopeful now that they were on their way. Staying in a grand old house might have its compensations and, after all, cousin Max would have grown up by now. Ant, too, began to ponder the possibilities. Meanwhile, Sloth the cat slumbered peacefully, dreaming only of a warm fire and the smell of fresh fish.

The train started to gather speed. The journey ahead was a long one. Ant and Sally sat back and stared out of the window, both lost in thought. What would the coming week hold in store?

After half an hour Sally got out some tapes. She was soon humming along to Peter Out and the Fadeaways. She played her entire collection twice, then tuned in to the radio. She learned some useful facts about ornamental hedge-clipping before switching off.

Ant whiled away the time with snacks from the buffet car. Then he practised a new card trick. After that, he counted fence posts flashing past the window. At 142, he gave up.

The journey became more and more boring. Only Sloth, snoring contentedly, seemed to be enjoying it. Station after station flashed past. Grime-caked chimneys gave way to thick, dark forests, then to bleak moorlands. Still the train rushed on, ever deeper into the countryside . . .

With a sudden jolt the train shuddered to a halt, the brakes screeching on the tracks. Ant and Sally woke with a start. The carriage was empty. They were the only passengers left on the train. They shivered in the icy air. It seemed to be much colder. Outside, the station name loomed out of the fog. This was it – the end of the line.

They stumbled onto the dark platform. The place was deserted. No ticket collector, no telephone, nothing but a single flickering light by the exit. They looked around uneasily as they waited . . . and waited.

A Twist of Fate

The fog swirled around them in chilly whorls, while the icy night air knifed through their clothes. Whichever way they looked, the road disappeared into inky blackness.

Suddenly, a shape loomed from the distant shadows. "Yoohoo!" Sally called, but her voice was lost in the rustling of tree branches blown and buffeted in a sudden angry breeze.

Was it imagination or did the shadowy stranger seem to beckon them to follow him?

Sinister shadows darted and flickered across their path as Ant and Sally chased after the caped figure. Moonlight glimmered through gaps in the scudding clouds. Tree branches clawed at the sky like bony fingers, while all around them they could hear faint rustling sounds from the undergrowth. Something swooped overhead – an owl scouring the ground in search of night-time prey, his yellow eyes glinting in anticipation.

Ant yelled and Sally shouted as they ran, but the fleeing shadow never stopped – or spoke. Then, gasping for breath, they rounded a corner and skidded to a halt. "He's gone," said Sally, in bewilderment, "Vanished!"

Ant didn't reply. He had spotted a battered old sign, half-hidden under a tangle of weeds. Crouching down, he wiped at its grimy surface with his sleeve. "Look," he said, staring at the shabby, peeling paintwork, "Gloomwood Road!"

Sally gasped with relief. By some strange twist of fate the caped stranger had led them to exactly where they wanted to be . . .

They fought their way along the weed-choked, unlit lane. At last they came to an imposing pillared gateway. Beyond it curved a long driveway. "This is it," said Sally, "Twelve Bells End!"

Daunted, they stared. Towering above them, stretching high into the
moonlit sky, was the dark and forbidding outline of an enormous house. Old
and neglected, only the occasional flickering light at a window showed that
someone lived there . . .

Journey's End

Sally lifted the heavy brass knocker on the front door. It hit the ancient wood with a loud, dull thud. There was a long pause, followed by the faint sound of approaching footsteps.

Stomachs churning, Ant and Sally watched the door handle begin to turn. Then a face poked slowly round the door frame.

Yeeees?

"Ha-ha-hallo," stuttered Sally. "W-w-w-we've come to stay. We g-g-got a letter . . . "

And then a second face popped out. At least this one looked jollier. "Hello!" it said, beaming. "You must be Sally and Anthony!"

The door opened wide and the owner of the face came forward with outstretched hands. "Pleased to meet you," he said, pumping Sally's arm up and down. "I'm Maximilian."

So *this* was their cousin Max. It was good to see a friendly face after that long dark walk.

Max turned to the frowning woman. "And this is Mrs Mopps, the housekeeper," he said. "Mrs Mopps, meet my cousins. They've come to stay."

"Will they be here long?" the housekeeper asked sourly, pursing her lips into a tight, straight line.

"About a week," answered Max. He beckoned to Ant and Sally to follow him inside the dark and uninviting house.

Ant and Sally hovered on the step then, gingerly, they stepped inside. The door clanged shut behind them.

They were in a narrow, musty corridor, dimly lit by dripping candles burning in ornate holders. Ahead, the sinister housekeeper slipped swiftly and silently away through the flickering shadows.

Nervously, they followed Max. What lay in store beyond the dark-panelled corridor?

"This is the main hallway," Max announced as they emerged from the dark and musty corridor. Stupefied, Ant and Sally stared around. Did people really live here? The place looked more like a museum than a house. It was a jumble of dusty portraits, ancient carvings, marble busts . . . And could that old man studying the globe really be one of their relatives?

Max hurried them towards a winding flight of stairs. Somewhere, far away in the house, a clock began to strike the hour. Sally shivered. It was colder inside this strange old house than it had been outside in the fog.

9

Surprises in Store

The ancient floorboards creaked and groaned under their feet as they climbed slowly up the stairs after Max. Outside, the wind moaned and sighed round the strange old house. The first drops of rain began to spatter against a cracked stained-glass window set deep into the wall.

At the top of the stairs, Sally clutched at the heavy wooden bannister. She gasped in disbelief. In front of her was a stout man on a unicycle. To her amazement, Max didn't seem to be surprised. "That's Mervin," he whispered to Ant and Sally, as the unicyclist sped past them and bumped his way down the stairs, "Your second cousin, twice removed."

Abruptly, Max turned left into a maze of dark, gloomy corridors, faintly lit by guttering candles. He led Ant and Sally through a huge stone archway into a vast gallery. "Here's the family!" he said.

From floor to ceiling, from centuries past to the present day, the entire Midnight family stared down at them. Before Ant and Sally could do more than glance around, Max hurried them on. But it seemed as if the eyes in every portrait swivelled and turned to follow them . . .

They went up some narrow, wooden stairs, then right along a corridor. At last Max stopped outside a gnarled oak door. He turned the handle. The door swung open. "Hope you like the room," said Max, disappearing.

With thudding hearts, Ant and Sally stepped inside. What more strange sights would this ancient and mysterious house reveal?

Dinner is at seven.

Shadows flickered in every corner. Outside, thunder grumbled angrily in the distance. A flash of lightning lit up the two chairs by the fire. Inside the house, a clock began to strike loudly. Ant looked at his watch: seven o'clock. Surely the clock had struck more than that?

CLANG! They spun round. The window was swinging wildly backwards and forwards, the glass rattling in the frame. WHOOSH! A blast of icy air swirled round the room. Then the window slammed shut again. The wind died away and the room became still.

The air felt strangely calm . . . until, from above the fireplace, came a faint rustling noise. Meanwhile, from far away, the booming sound of a gong reverberated through the house. The rustling noise grew gradually louder. Ant and Sally stood, rooted to the spot. One by one, page after page was tearing off the calendar and spinning dizzily round the room.

Dinner is Served . . .

With mounting trepidation Ant and Sally made their way downstairs. The sound of babbling voices led them to the dining room. Nervously, they pushed the door open and went inside.

Gaping they stared around. Then Max ushered them towards two empty chairs. And so began the strangest evening of their lives. All they could do was watch and listen . . .

SOME VERY PECULIAR PEOPLE INDEED WERE SCRUTINIZING THEM IN STONY SILENCE.

Mysterious Messages

At last, Ant and Sally made their escape. Back in their room, they shut the door with relief. Max had promised an action-packed schedule for the following day but, for the moment at least, they were alone.

"What a place," said Ant, "And what a meal!"

"What on earth is going on?" said Sally, slumping into a chair. "And why is everyone so strange?"

Ant decided to tackle the most pressing problem. Fortunately, he had emergency rations at hand. He tore the wrapping off a packet of biscuits and they munched their way through it, then another . . . and then a third.

Outside the weather was worsening. The strengthening wind howled down the chimney and driving rain lashed viciously at the windows. With sinking hearts, they got ready for bed. But they were in for a shock. So far, nothing in that strange old house had been quite what they expected – and their room was no exception.

The old house creaked and groaned as the ancient timbers settled for the night. Moonlight threw flickering shadows on to the walls and floor. Ant and Sally shivered under the icy bedclothes. They heard the sound of feet padding stealthily along the corridor. Did the footsteps stop outside their door? It was hard to be sure . . . At last they drifted off into uneasy sleep.

Little did they know that, while they slept, strange forces were at work in the old house. When all was dark and quiet, somewhere, the clock struck midnight. Inside the room nothing stirred. Then, from the floor, came a faint rustling noise. The scattered calendar leaves started to gather together, then flew up the chimney, vanishing without a sound.

14

Sally stirred restlessly. Was a faint faraway voice whispering her name? "Sally, Sally, wake up!" the eerie voice seemed to say, over and over again.

Ant rolled over, half asleep, half awake. Was a cold, clammy hand really clutching and clawing at his shoulder, shaking him into consciousness?

Quivering with fear and wide awake, they both sat bolt upright. "W-what's happening?" said Ant, clutching the bedclothes tightly around him.

"I d-don't know," said Sally, staring wildly around the room. "But I don't think I like it."

CRASH! A notebook flew off the shelf and landed, open, on the floor. Sloth jumped off the bed, yeowling with terror. He stood over the book, hissing and spitting, back arched and fur bristling. Ant and Sally watched, horror-struck, as wavering lines slowly appeared on the empty page – lines that spelled out just one single word.

CRRRRK! The door to the wardrobe started to open. Groaning and complaining, it swung slowly outwards. Then a message started to appear on the mirror. With unsteady strokes, word after word started to form before their eyes. Quaking with fright they saw that the words spelled out a desperate warning. But what did it mean?

WOOOOOOAHH! A blast of icy wind swept round the room and swirled into the fireplace. It caught up a bundle of paper scrumpled in the grate. Flapping and billowing, the paper unfolded. Ant and Sally were too terrified to move or speak. In front of them were the faded pages of an ancient newspaper.

Trembling, Sally picked up the crumpled, yellowing paper and spread it out on the floor in front of her.

HAVOC HITS HISTORIC HOUSE!

Exposed: *the chilling secrets of Twelve Bells End — house of horror!*

From our correspondent
BILLY VITTORNOT

THE LATEST in a series of freak accidents to hit residents of Twelve Bells End happened at midnight last night when a man was badly concussed by a jar of pickled onions.

The accident happened when his cycle was in collision with the back of a van carrying groceries for the Pricewar chain of supermarkets. The cycle was split in two by the accident and the man was rushed to the casualty department of Gallstone General Hospital.

The man, a bachelor (43), was later named as Mervin Midnight of Twelve Bells End. He is said to be stable and asking for his bicycle.

Dogged by misfortune

THIS IS NOT the first time tragedy has hit Twelve Bells End. In a chain of bizarre coincidences many residents have suffered accidents resulting in personality changes and memory loss.

Victims of fate

ATTRACTIVE brunette Posy Tutu (39), once principal soloist with the Bolshy Ballet, was dropped in mid pas-de-deux by her leading man. The incident happened during a production staged at Twelve Bells End. Since then, Miss Tutu has hung up her ballet shoes and is now a regular at the Middle-Knight Junior soccer try-outs.

Merry prankster Juster Chuckle was once well-known for his practical jokes and hilarious one-liners — until he nearly died laughing. One night, while telling his favourite joke, the young wag laughed himself breathless, then fainted. Upon recovery, Chuckle was so shaken by the incident that he vowed never to laugh again. To avoid an accidental rib-tickler, he now speaks sentences backwards only. He plans to become a mathematics teacher.

LATEST VICTIM: Mervin Midnight

SOCCER-CRAZY: Posy Tutu

TEEN-SCREAM TURNED TEACH: Chuckle

Midnight mansion

TWELVE BELLS END has been in the Midnight family for generations. The house was designed by the first Lord Midnight who drew heavily on his travels abroad for inspiration.

Inferno

THIRTY years ago yesterday, the house narrowly escaped destruction in a fire

Fire drama mansion

which swept through part of the east wing. The only victim was the twelfth Lord Midnight, despite vain attempts to save him by plucky local man Frank Forthright.

Also on the scene was Fireman Slift. Slift commented: "Lord Midnight seemed to be delirious towards the end. His last words were: 'A custard mouse and door to swallow me'."

WIN, WIN, WIN!

in the

SCORCHER

big cash bonanza!

Local lore: house is jinxed

*Our reporter **MAY KITTUP** has been on the spot to gauge local reaction to this latest tragic event*

THE SLEEPY VILLAGE of Middle-Knight-on-Sea is buzzing with talk of the strange goings-on at Twelve Bells End.

It seems that many villagers have long held the belief that the house is under some kind of jinx. Yet there was a strange reluctance on the part of most of the villagers to talk. One local man finally consented to meet me – but insisted he remain anonymous. We met under a small shrub in the car park behind the Spectre and Stone public house. Mr X seemed shifty and ill-at-ease while we spoke.

Local councillor Polly Bellowes, a familiar figure around the village

Village of fear

"They say there's rooms in that house have been empty and locked for years," Mr X claimed, checking around him nervously. "And once a year," he added in a whisper, "They say a caped figure paces the corridors, moaning and wailing and wringing his hands." With this, Mr X refused to say more and left.

Lone voice

ONE VILLAGER who doesn't share the general fears is Councillor Polly Bellowes. She scoffs at suggestions that the house might be cursed. "People round here," she commented, "Spend too much time in idle gossip." Following the latest accident, she has called for an enquiry into road maintenance policy.

My flaming battle!

*Thirty years on, have-a-go hero Frank Forthright talks exclusively to the **SCORCHER** about his bold rescue bid*

SHY FRANK, a confirmed bachelor (52), was unwilling to talk at first. "Why bring

all that up? – it's history," commented the reluctant hero. He added, "I tried to save him – even he deserved a chance."

When asked if he could shed further light on Lord Midnight's last words, Mr Forthright became agitated and asked our reporter to leave. He declined to make any further comment.

Village of Fear

The next day dawned bright and sunny. Shafts of light beamed in through the old mullioned window in their room. Had the events of the night before ever really happened? It seemed hard to believe.

"I'm hungry," said Ant. "Let's go to the village." Sally agreed, glad to avoid another meal in the mysterious old house.

Quietly, they let themselves out of the front door and set off down the driveway.

At the end of Gloomwood Road they turned left. In the distance they could see clusters of houses huddled together, hugging the curves of the road as it twisted and turned on its way to the sea.

Walking towards the straggling outskirts of the village, an old woman stopped them. Slyly, she looked at Ant, then Sally.

"We don't like strangers here," she hissed. "You'd best be going." And with that, she scuttled away.

Taken aback, Ant and Sally walked slowly on. Ten minutes later they reached the village. But in the narrow high street they became uncomfortably aware of a great deal of attention . . .

The further into the village they went, the more the sensation grew. Heads swivelled furtively to watch them. Prying eyes bored into their backs. Faces peered out from behind twitching curtains. But no one spoke a word to them – or almost no one.

Just then Ant felt an urgent tug at his sleeve. The anxious voice of an old man whispered in his ear. "You be the guests up at Twelve Bells End? Go! Leave while there's still time!" But before they could reply, he had fled.

Ant and Sally stared at each other. It hardly seemed possible. The entire village was scared to death . . . but why?

Nervously, they opened the door to the village store. The tinny bell rang out. Everyone inside the tiny shop turned to stare. Then there was silence.

"Here long?" the shopkeeper said at last.

"A week," Sally answered, to a sharp intake of breath from one of the customers.

"Are you sure that's wise?" asked the shopkeeper, heavily.

Ant hastily chose a packet of strawberry-flavoured Scrunchy-Munchies, then they paid up and left. But once they were outside the shop, they heard an urgent hissing noise behind them. They swivelled round . . .

For a moment, Ant and Sally thought they were hearing things. But there was no doubt about it, someone lurking behind the wall was trying to attract their notice.

"There's someone you should meet – who knows more than he tells," whispered the anonymous voice. "Follow this road to the green, then look for the cottage with red windows. It's next to a blue cottage, on a slight hill. But hurry!"

Across the busy green they could see the house, just as the mystery voice had described it. They hesitated. What would lie in wait for them there?

The Story Unfolds . . .

Quaking slightly, Ant and Sally walked up the path to the cottage. Suddenly, there was a shout from the garden. Startled, they turned. A red-faced figure was approaching, brandishing his walking stick at them.

"Hullo. W-we're staying at T-Twelve Bells End," Sally babbled. The figure shuffled nearer. He seemed faintly familiar, somehow. Had they seen him somewhere before?

Then they recognized him. Advancing on them was a portlier, older version of heroic Frank Forthright from the newspaper. So *this* was who they had been sent to meet! But why?

Should I warn them?

Frank stared at them. He seemed agitated and about to speak, then changed his mind. He shuffled from foot to foot. At last he spoke. "Leave now," he said slowly. "No good will come of staying."

Then Ant butted in. "Please help us. There are strange things going on – things we can't explain," he said, "In the house, in the village . . . and our relatives . . . "

"Relatives?" interrupted Frank sharply. "You're members of the Midnight family?"

"Yes," said Ant, bewildered. "Why?"

Frank seemed deep in thought. Then, with a heavy sigh, he spoke. "You'd better come inside. There are things you need to know."

He beckoned Ant and Sally to follow him up the path. Inside the house, he led them to a small sitting room and gestured to three threadbare chairs ranged around the empty fireplace. "Sit down," he said, "And listen hard to what I have to say."

"Twelve Bells End is an evil place," he began. "It all started the night the fire broke out in the east wing many years ago . . . "

20

21

The Midnight Stone

There was a moment's silence as Frank's tale reached its chilling conclusion. Then Ant ventured, "The Stone? What Stone?"

Frank reached up to the bookshelf and took down a heavy old tome, covered with years of dust and grime.

---

112 GREAT GEMS OF THE WORLD

The Midnight Stone

Property of the Midnight family, the Stone forms the centrepiece of a magnificent relic (pictured right). Intricately fashioned in pewter with rubies inset on the base, the relic has a matched pair of Loukaniki goats* ornately detailed on the upper surface. The Stone itself is made of cyanozine, one of the world's rarest minerals.

An artist's impression of the Midnight Stone and relic

Lord Midnight decreed that the Stone should forever stay within the Midnight family and never be sold

Origins of the Stone

The Stone came into the Midnight family after the first Lord Midnight, an intrepid explorer, discovered Mythika, a hitherto unknown country. Lord Midnight quickly became a favourite at the court of Queen Fatima (see opposite). A gifted linguist, he soon spoke fluent Mythikan, including seven regional dialects.

Alas, upon suggesting it was time for him to return to his native land, Queen Fatima clapped him in a dungeon. His only food was grilled lizards and pureed slugs, fed to him once a day through his prison bars.

The court jester, however, owed Lord Midnight a deep debt of gratitude. Some weeks earlier Lord Midnight had spoken eloquently in favour of a rise in basic wages for Fools. This had resulted in payment of an extra two olives per year for the jester.

When the jester overheard Fatima planning to execute Lord Midnight the following day, he plotted a daring jail break. The escape went as planned. As Lord Midnight prepared to flee the jester handed him the relic as a parting gift.

Lord Midnight bids farewell to the noble jester

Reproduction of a woodcut by Athos of Pathos

© MOMMA (Museum of Medieval Mythikan Art)

* Loukanikis are native only to Mythika. They are the country's national emblem.

"There," he said, jabbing a bony forefinger at the page they should read. "The Midnight Stone. Famed for its beauty and fated from the day it fell into the hands of the Midnight family!"

Ant and Sally were soon engrossed in the strange history of the ancient gem. Sloth, not such a keen historian, stalked off for a tour of the kitchen. When they finished reading, Frank closed the book, saying solemnly, "But that's not all. The story of the Stone doesn't end there!"

Historic Background to Stone

Lord Midnight, a keen diarist and amateur artist of some distinction, has left a source of valuable information about the Mythikan culture and people. Below are extracts from his jottings, with explanatory notes.

She seemeth a goodlye sorte of monarche

An excerpt from Lord Midnight's diary

the foole hath warned me not to lette it slippe into the wronge handes - for he sayeth it supporteth the moste strange and fantastik poweres.

1) Fatima (pictured above by Lord Midnight) is now widely regarded as one of the harshest Mythikan rulers. Mythikans were expected to perform continuous athletic feats, such as triple somersaults, back flips and handstands, while in her presence. Only those over ninety-five were exempt from this ruling.

2) For many centuries it was the duty of the jester to make up a new joke every hour. If the joke failed to make the ruling monarch laugh, the points on the jester's cap and shoes would be ceremonially snipped off with a pair of hedge clippers.

In addition, it was the traditional role of the jester to act as guardian of the relic. We have no record of what happened to the jester befriended by Lord Midnight.

A Family Scandal

Frank's eyes misted over as he started to recall the fateful events that followed in the history of the Stone. "It all took place one ordinary autumn afternoon," he began, "Two weeks before the fire that claimed the twelfth Lord Midnight . . ."

A Walk through the Woods

At last Frank concluded his mysterious tale. "That's all I can tell you," he said, slumping back in the shabby chair. "Now go. Take the short cut through the gate at the end of the road and go round the lake. But hurry!"

Ant and Sally stood up to go. Exhausted, Frank mopped at his brow with a large spotted handkerchief. "They say the one who finds the Stone can lift the curse," he continued weakly. "And that there's a secret room in the house that holds the key to the whereabouts of the Stone. Now leave me be – for it's rumoured that any who help those who meddle with the Midnight Stone may, too, fall foul of the curse!"

Ant and Sally hurried down the road, heads reeling. Could they really be staying in a house under the threat of an ancient curse? And who, they wondered uneasily, would the next victim be?

"How on earth do we find the Stone?" said Sally. "It's been missing for years."

Something about the story was niggling Ant. It was something the twelfth Lord Midnight had said when he cursed the house: "So long as the Stone is mine" ... Why should he call the Stone *mine*, when his twin brother had stolen it? After all, the Stone had never been recovered.

Before Sally could reply, they reached the gate at the end of the road. Lifting the ancient latch, they pushed hard against the rotting wood. The hinges whined once in protest, then they were through.

Dense trees stretched above them, cutting out all but the faintest glimmer of sunshine. Half-blinded by the sudden change from light to shade, Ant and Sally hesitated a moment. Then, slowly, their eyes adjusted to the gloom ...

What kind of place was this? Neglected for years, the stench of rot and decay was overpowering. No birds sang, no wind rustled the leaves, not a ripple disturbed the dank, dark water of the lake. Hearts pounding, Ant and Sally stumbled along the slippery bank. Branches scratched at their faces, brambles clutched at their feet, and then the path petered out. They were surrounded by an army of tall trees. It was impossible to tell which way to go. "We're lost," gulped Sally.

A cold, clammy feeling crawled up Ant's spine. A quiet voice had whispered his name, but there was no one in sight. Then, through the trees, Ant saw a dark, silent figure, beckoning them to follow him.

Ant and Sally struggled to keep up with the shadowy stranger who led them through the dark woods. His cape swirled round him as he moved. His feet seemed hardly to touch the ground as he glided silently onwards . . .

The Missing Window

Chinks of sunlight filtered through the trees. Ant and Sally could hear birds twittering in the distance. Then, blinking in the sudden light, they were out of the woods and on the edge of the garden. But there was no sign of the strange and shadowy figure who had led them from the lake. He had vanished as mysteriously as he had appeared.

They scanned the scene in front of them. The garden, still sodden from the heavy rain of the night, stretched away in front of them. In every corner they could see familiar faces from the meal of the evening before.

The morning sun glinted palely on the old house. The ancient stones had mellowed down the ages to a soft shade of grey. Sally peered at the first-floor windows and tried to work out which belonged to their room. The more she looked, the more something struck her as strange – but what was it?

Of course! Clutching Ant's arm, she spluttered, "Look! Next to our room. There was a window there once. Could there be a room behind it?"

They sprinted across the garden. Would they find a secret room? And could it hold a vital clue to the whereabouts of the Stone, as Frank had said?

They pounded up the steps, wrenched the back door open and thundered through the house. In frantic haste, they searched the length of the corridor outside their room. Surely there must be a door here somewhere?

Unknown to them, they were not alone in the dark and gloomy corridor. A lurking figure was watching every move they made and listening hard to every word they said . . .

Then Sally had a brainwave. Panting, they moved a heavy cabinet that was jutting out from the wall. Behind it, festooned in cobwebs, was a door!

Neither of them had heard the faint rustling of a starched skirt, nor noticed the sound of hurried footsteps disappearing round the corner . . .

Behind the Locked Door

With trembling hands, Sally grasped the key. It was almost jammed solid in the lock. At last, with a loud click, it turned. Ant pushed against the door. The age-old hinges, unoiled and unused for years, creaked into life.

It was like stepping into another world. Ant and Sally gaped, dumbfounded. Magnificent objects were crammed into every corner of the room. Exotic carvings jostled for space on ornate furniture. A fabulously coloured tapestry hung lopsidedly from the wall. And was that some kind of musical instrument strung from the hook in the corner?

No one had been inside the room for years. A film of dust lay over every surface. The room smelt musty. No breeze stirred the air, no sunlight lit the shadows that lurked in every corner.

The only sound in the ancient room was the slow, rhythmic tick of a large clock standing by the wall. How strange that it should still be going after all these years . . .

All of a sudden, the clock whirred and clanked into action. It began to strike the hour. One . . . Two . . . Three . . . Four . . . Five . . . Six . . . Seven . . . Eight . . . Nine . . . Ten . . . Eleven . . . Twelve . . .

The echo of the last stroke died away. Ant looked at his watch. "Twelve?" he said, puzzled. Then the door into the room slammed shut behind them.

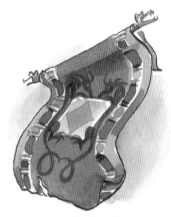

The musical instrument in the corner swung slowly on its hook. One by one the rusted old strings began to tauten, then break. A strange-looking statue, perched on a table, jerked slowly into action. Round and round it danced as if by clockwork. Then the old scroll hanging from the wall started to flap and flutter on its hook.

"W-what's happening?" said Sally. A cold breath brushed the back of her neck. She cowered against the door, shivering with fright.

Sudden sunlight pierced the gloom. It was as if shafts of bright light were streaming in through a window – a window that was no longer there. Then a blast of icy air howled into the room and whistled past Ant and Sally.

CLUNK! The wind snatched a book from the bookcase. The heavy tome fell to the floor with a thud. A shower of dust flew out of its crinkled pages.

The brilliant shaft of light blazed down on the old book. The wind whirled round and round it in angry gusts. Could the ancient pages hold some kind of clue to the mystery?

Sally bent to pick up the book. The wind died away and, for a moment, all was silent.

SSSSS! From the corner, there was a faint hissing, whining noise. It grew louder and louder. Ant and Sally span round. The noise was coming from an old-fashioned radio perched on a table in the corner.

Stone . . . Hurry . . .
Read the diary . . .
But beware . . .
Enemy in house . . .
Hurry . . .

The radio started to crackle into life. Quietly, so quietly that at first they couldn't make out the words, a faint, disembodied voice began to speak . . .

31

Max Takes Charge

A nt and Sally shot out of the room as fast as their wobbling legs would let them. Sally was still clutching the book she had picked up. "Look," she gasped. "It's a diary . . . Remember the radio message!" They stared at the battered old book. Could a vital clue to the missing Stone lurk in its dusty pages? Just then they heard footsteps approaching.

Beaming proudly, Max appeared round the corner. He was full of his plans for the day. Ant and Sally were aghast. But there was no escape.

Following Max's wobbly lead they headed down the winding lane on the ancient trikes he had dug out for them. At the village cafe, Max suggested they stop and have lunch. He was soon tucking in to a generous portion of gooseberry tartlet with spicy tomato relish.

Time ticked away. Ant's burger turned cold on its plate. Sally's sandwich curled up at the corners. Would Max never finish eating? They must find the Stone before the ancient curse claimed its next victim!

With a sigh of pleasure Max mopped the last traces of tomato off his chin. "Let's go!" he said. Ant and Sally jumped up. Free at last! But Max had plenty more entertainment in store back at Twelve Bells End.

Out in the garden Max began to explain the finer points of the first game. Ant racked his brains for a way to sound him out about the Stone. At last he blurted out a question, but Max ignored him. It was as if he hadn't heard a word Ant said.

Max seemed to find nothing strange about the games he had organized. Spin the Potty was followed by some slug racing. After a nail-biting finish Sally's slug, Desmond, was declared the winner. He was awarded a rosette.

Game followed game. Would they ever manage to get away? They played Hunt the Tarantula, Pass the Partridge, Hide and Squeak . . . Then, at last, dusk started to fall.

The first violent sheets of rain were lashing down on to the garden as they headed inside. Max had a musical evening planned. He performed movingly on the harp then led everyone in some spirited singing.

Sally looked anxiously at her watch. "We *must* read the diary," she hissed to Ant under cover of a noisy sea shanty. "Time is running out!"

33

The Diary

Half an hour later Ant and Sally managed to get away. They rushed back to their room. Sally picked up the diary. It fell open at the final entry and several bits of paper dropped out. They proved to be some very interesting bits of paper indeed . . .

FLOGGIT & QUICK

Valuation: Midnight Stone

Estimated resale value:
— Stone   £7,300
— Stone   £10,560
  in setting

Less our commission @ 40%

Total: £4,380
— Stone   £6,336
— Stone
  in setting

'Tis passing strange they have noe P nor X

Purchase - mandolin String, leeches, red hose

Top cop cops it!

Inspector Smug, the Yard's newest recruit, has been at the centre of a major scandal this week. This follows complaints of unlawful arrest by 42 members of the public in the last three months.

Smug admits to an arrest rate over 37% above the force average. The cuff-happy cop, whose previous jobs included a spell as quality controller for Tuffaware All-Weather Anoraks, transferred to the force seven years ago. A rapid rise through the ranks led to his promotion early last year.

A spokesman commented: "It happens sometimes. You get these newly promoted officers, keen as mustard – and a bit high-handed. The officer in question has been severely reprimanded."

SMUG: too eager

Happy days for my Darling sons on the lake

This one looks promising!

The wind howled round the house and thunder grumbled angrily in the distance while they pored over the diary. Sloth prowled around the room, hissing uneasily, but they hardly noticed. Then something caught Sally's eye. "Look," she said excitedly, "Look at the date of the diary entry!"

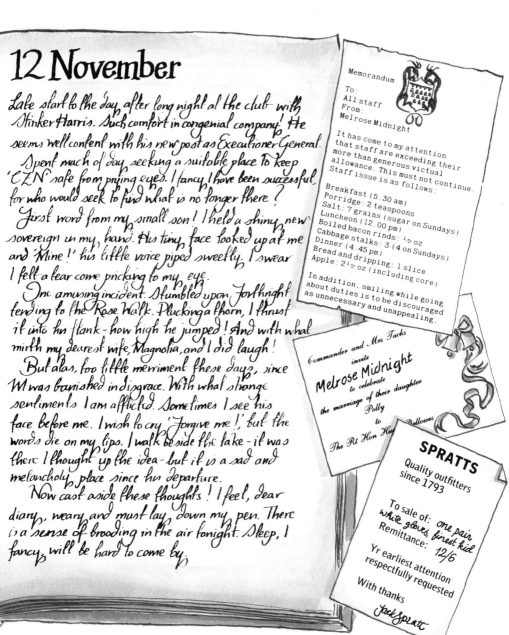

12 November

Late start to the day, after long night at the club with Stinker Harris. Such comfort in congenial company! He seems well content with his new post as Executioner General.

Spent much of day, seeking a suitable place to keep 'CZN' safe from prying eyes. I fancy I have been successful, for who would seek to find what is no longer there?

First word from my small son! I held a shiny new sovereign in my hand. His tiny face looked up at me and 'Mine!' his little voice piped sweetly. I swear I felt a tear come pricking to my eye.

One amusing incident. Stumbled upon Forthnight tending to the Rose Walk. Plucking a thorn, I thrust it into his flank – how high he jumped! And with what mirth my dearest wife, Magnolia, and I did laugh!

But alas, too little merriment these days, since M was banished in disgrace. With what strange sentiments I am afflicted. Sometimes I see his face before me. I wish to cry 'Forgive me!', but the words die on my lips. I walk beside the lake – it was there I thought up the idea – but it is a sad and melancholy place since his departure.

Now cast aside these thoughts! I feel, dear diary, weary and must lay down my pen. There is a sense of brooding in the air tonight. Sleep, I fancy, will be hard to come by.

Memorandum

To: All staff
From: Melrose Midnight

It has come to my attention that staff are exceeding their more than generous victual allowance. This must not continue. Staff issue is as follows:

Breakfast (5.30 am)
Porridge: 2 teaspoons
Salt: 7 grains (sugar on Sundays)
Luncheon (12.00 pm)
Boiled bacon rinds: ½ oz
Cabbage stalks: 3 (4 on Sundays)
Dinner (4.45 pm)
Bread and dripping: 1 slice
Apple: 2½ oz (including core)

In addition, smiling while going about duties is to be discouraged as unnecessary and unappealing.

Commander and Mrs Jacks
invite
Melrose Midnight
to celebrate
the marriage of their daughter
Polly
to
The Rt Hon Hu___ ___llowes

SPRATTS
Quality outfitters
since 1793

To sale of: one pair white gloves, finest kid
Remittance: 12/6

Yr earliest attention respectfully requested

With thanks

Jack Spratt

The Pointing Finger

A nt looked at the date on the final diary entry. Something about the date jogged his memory. Of course! Suddenly it all fell into place . . . The twelfth of November: the night of the fire, the night the twelfth Lord Midnight put the curse on the house . . . The twelfth of November: the night of cousin Mervin's accident, and of Aunt Posy's – and of all the other accidents to members of the Midnight family . . . They all happened on the twelfth of November, and all at midnight!

"But," faltered Ant, "That's today's date. We've only got two hours left to find the Stone and break the curse before it happens again!"

Little did Ant and Sally know that the sinister housekeeper was skulking outside the door. With her ear glued to the keyhole, she could hear every word they said . . .

Then, from down the corridor, there was a faint whirring noise. The clock in the secret room once more started to strike.

Inside their room Ant and Sally hardly noticed the distant noise. Desperately they scoured the final diary entry for clues.

Ant had a thought. The Stone was made from cyanozine. Could "CZN" be a secret code for the Stone? But then what was the meaning of ". . . for who seeks to find what is no longer there"?

DONG! The hidden clock struck twelve. Sally felt an idea starting to form.

The secret room . . . The room that "is no longer there"!

They must have missed something. The clue to the Stone *had* to be in the secret room. They must go back!

If Ant and Sally had listened, they would have heard the sound of pounding feet running away. But they had forgotten about the crackling message on the radio, about the voice that warned them of an enemy in the house.

36

Outside the house, the rain battered against the ancient brickwork. A loud clap of thunder shook the old stone walls. Inside the hidden room, the temperature was icy. But was it only the cold that made them shiver as they looked around the dark and gloomy room?

All of a sudden, two ancient candles encrusted with age-old drips of wax, burst into flame. Sinister shadows and shapes filled the room, darting and flickering into every corner. Sally quivered with fear. Had a strange shadowy figure just flitted past her? And was that a faint voice whispering her name? "Sally, Sally. Turn round . . . Face the portrait. Look at the portrait."

With a terrified shudder, Sally turned to face the portrait. Staring down from the grimy frame were two figures: twin brothers . . .

Sally gasped. Was it a trick of the light or had the figures just moved? Then the figures moved again. Now one of the twins was pointing urgently at a statue. Meanwhile, the other twin scowled down with an expression of great menace.

Sally had seen the statue in the portrait before, in the garden. Could this be the end of the trail at last? Did the answer to the disappearance of the ancient gem lie outside in the wild and stormy night?

A Cryptic Clue

The wind howled and shrieked through the trees as Ant and Sally raced down the garden. Driving rain lashed at their faces. Above them, swollen thunderclouds scudded angrily through the stormy skies.

A flash of lightning seared across the dark and sinister garden. Ahead, glimmering eerily in the stormy light, they could see the ancient statue. Would this be the end of their search? They ran towards it. Then a giant burst of thunder crashed and rolled round the garden.

The cold, unblinking eyes of the old stone statue stared straight ahead as, with freezing fingers, they prodded and poked in every nook and cranny. Water trickled down their necks and seeped up through their shoes. They grew icy cold. It was hopeless. There was no sign of the ancient stone.

"Let's go back," shouted Sally above the noise of the wailing wind and swaying trees. "There's nothing here!" But speeding back to the house through the menacing shadows, neither of them noticed what a strange time of night it was for a woodcutter to be at work . . .

Back inside the secret room, dripping and chilled to the bone, they racked their brains desperately. Had they, somewhere, missed a clue? Ant stared at the portrait. A glimmer of an idea was forming in his head. "Maybe," he said slowly, "The figure isn't pointing at the statue at all . . ."

Maybe the figure is pointing at the frame itself!

There's something stuck in the back!

The moment Ant spoke, the picture started to shake and rattle on its hook. It shuddered from side to side, as if it was locked in some violent battle. Sally stretched up and grabbed the edges of the frame, then heaved as hard as she could. Tottering, she lowered the picture off the wall. With trembling fingers, she levered the back away from the frame. And there, wedged inside was a dusty piece of paper, tightly folded.

Ant lifted the paper out and unfolded it. The crinkled old sheet felt as if it might crumble to bits in his hands. Gingerly, he smoothed it out and stared down at the torn sheet. The spindly handwriting was all too familiar to both of them . . . They began to read. Would this, at last, lead them to the hiding place of the Midnight Stone?

Of many sides but single voice,
In rhythm but no rhyme,
Once hear me sing and you will find
I hold the key to time.

Bewildered, they reached the end of the mysterious message. It was some kind of poem, but it seemed to make no sense. What could it mean?

Outside, the wind still raged round the old house. It tore some old slate tiles from the roof and flung them to the ground, shattering them into tiny pieces. And all the while, time was edging closer and closer to midnight .

The End of the Search

A deafening roll of thunder shook the old house to its foundations. Ant and Sally huddled, shivering, inside the secret room. Again and again they read through the puzzling lines of the strange poem.

What was it they should look for? Something that could sing? Could that mean a musical instrument? But something with many sides? Was there anything inside this room that fitted that description? . . . At the same moment they both sprang into action.

There was no time to lose. Frantically, they searched the room. It *had* to be in here. But they found nothing. Then, almost despairing, Sally picked up a six-sided brown box and opened the lid .

At once, the eerie strains of a scraping stringed instrument filled the room. It was unlike anything Ant or Sally had heard before. Inside the box, sad-faced figures looped and twirled to the mournful tune.

Ant and Sally stood spellbound. Then a faint voice whispered, "It's a trick! Don't listen to the music."

Ant blinked. Something glinted inside the box. And there, cleverly hidden, was "the key to time"!

Now, should you seek a hiding place
These lines shall hold the answer.
Look for the courtier who ne'er
A step doth take, though dancer.

There, cloak'd in velvet secrecy,
Lies cloister'd from all sight
A precious stone, whose colour hides
Deeds darker than the night.

Ant grabbed the key. But what did it open? . . . Of course! He ran over to the clock. Fumbling, he pushed the key into the lock and turned it. The door swung open. Inside, the pendulum ticked slowly from side to side. Tucked away, they could see the edge of another torn sheet of paper.

Sally pulled it out. It was the rest of the riddle! They puzzled over the cryptic lines. Then they heard a faint voice urge, "Over here! Over here!"

BANG! The clock door slammed shut. The lights began to flicker. Then a sharp hissing noise, like an angry intake of breath, echoed round the room. But above the noise they heard the faint voice still calling to them. Ant and Sally span round towards the voice. Immediately Ant spotted something. "Look. The courtier!" he gasped.

Ant picked up the statue from the chest. He turned it over and over in his hands. But where was the Stone? There seemed to be no possible hiding place.

WOOOSH! A violent gust of icy wind swept the statue out of his hands. It crashed on to the floor and split in two – and there was something hidden inside . . .

Peeking out from between the two shattered halves was the corner of a dark blue velvet bag. Sally grabbed it. Trembling, she untied the knot.

Her fingers scrabbled inside the opened bag. She touched something – something cold as marble, smooth as silk. With trembling hands, she pulled it out of the bag . . .

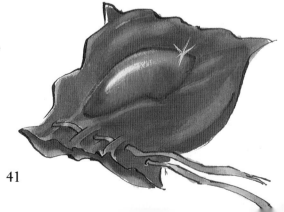

41

Chaos Reigns

They had found the Midnight Stone at last! They stood marvelling at its dazzling beauty. Shimmering lights in shades of blue glowed off its smooth surface. But could they return the Stone to its rightful resting place before the final stroke of midnight? There were just five minutes left.

"Follow me," said Sally. Clutching the precious stone, she raced down into the hallway. There, perched high above them on the wall, was the relic.

It was hopeless. Sally's fingers groped helplessly just a few inches out of reach of the relic. But help was at hand. At that moment the professor came down the stairs. Anxiously, Sally held out the Stone. Smiling, he took it. Then chaos broke out.

KERRANG! A mirror flew off the wall and shattered on the floor. Sloth began to yowl. A great wind whistled into the hallway. It circled and whirled around the professor in violent gusts, spinning him round and round like a helpless toy top.

The noise was deafening. And, above it all, Sally thought she could hear a faint ghostly cry. But was it a cry of triumph or of anger?

The great wind howled round the hallway like some maddened wild beast. Outside a fork of lightning streaked past the window. They heard a mighty cracking noise. An ancient oak, standing sentinel for centuries past, had crashed to the ground.

DONG! Far away in the secret room, the clock started to chime. And on the twelfth stroke, the ancient curse would claim another victim . . .

Suddenly, a dark shadow loomed towards Ant, Sally and the professor. They cowered away, horror-struck. A sinister figure they recognized only too well moved nearer and nearer, arms outstretched to grab at the Stone . . .

A Sorry Tale

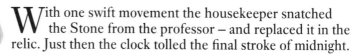

With one swift movement the housekeeper snatched the Stone from the professor – and replaced it in the relic. Just then the clock tolled the final stroke of midnight.

"No-o-o!" A ghostly howl of despair filled the hallway. Everyone stood immobile, chilled to the bone by the unearthly scream that ricocheted from wall to wall. Then the final anguished echoes faded away and all was silent.

Ant and Sally shivered. A faint, whispering voice, a whispering voice they had both heard before, began to echo through the hallway. "At last, at last, at last!", the faint voice whispered triumphantly, before it too died away.

For a moment everyone was dumbstruck, too dazed to move or speak . . . or almost everyone.

Stop him! He's a villain and an impostor!

44

What Happened Next . . .

The housekeeper smiled. "My name is Marcia Midnight," she began. "My father was Maurice, disinherited twin brother of the twelfth Lord Midnight."

"When my father was banished, accused of stealing the Stone, he went to Mythika," she continued. "He got a job there as a lifeguard. That's how he met my mother. He saved her when a sea urchin punctured her water wings. They married within a fortnight. A year later, I was born. I was their only child."

Marcia Midnight rummaged in her apron and proudly produced a framed snapshot.

"My father never talked of the past," she went on. "Until, just before he died, he told me of his suspicions of his brother's treachery. I vowed to find proof to clear my father's name. I saw the job as housekeeper advertised. It seemed the perfect cover for some sleuthing. That was five months ago."

Tell me, Mrs Mopps, have you had much experience of French polishing?

"I soon realized that some strange spell hung over the people in the house. Then I stumbled on some papers that showed someone was stealing from each and every inmate. But who? The crook had covered his tracks well."

Marcia Midnight sat back exhausted, then continued. "Was there, I wondered, some connection between the strange spell and the fraud?"

"When you two arrived I put you in the room that the twelfth Lord Midnight and my father shared when they were boys. And that's when things started happening. From then on I followed your every move. The diary you found cleared my father's name. But there was no time to reveal the truth. The Stone had to be found! Then the professor made his fatal mistake . . ."

A cape!

The caped stranger!

Marcia Midnight dabbed at her eyes with a fine linen handkerchief, then spoke again. "Now my father is at peace, thanks to you. I know he would want you to have this."

She handed Ant and Sally a bulky bundle. "It was his favourite garment," she said, with a small and mysterious smile . . .

The next day Ant and Sally woke late. They dressed quickly and went downstairs. Max was alone in the dining room, sitting at the huge oval table. "Morning," he said. "Come and have some breakfast."

Ant and Sally sat down. They gaped around them at the transformation. Gone were the peculiar meals of the last few days. On the table were fruit juices, toast, cereal . . . And Max sat chewing on a croissant as if the strange and sinister events of the last few days had never taken place.

"All back to normal then?" asked Ant. But Max just looked at him blankly.

And whoever they spoke to, it was the same story. No one seemed to know what they were talking about. Posy Tutu was back at the barre, cousin Mervin was balancing his books . . . Everyone was behaving just as if nothing had happened. They didn't appear to remember anything at all.

Ant and Sally stared at each other, confused. Had it all been a dream?

Then Marcia Midnight appeared. "Follow me," she said, beckoning.

She led them to the secret room. But now the door was scrubbed. A shiny key twinkled in the lock. Inside, the window had been replaced. Beams of sunlight streamed on to furniture gleaming with polish. The place was spotless.

"There's something I thought you'd like to see," said Marcia Midnight. And then once more she smiled . . .

Did You Spot?

You can use this page to help you spot things that could be useful in solving the mystery. First, there are hints and clues you can read as you go along. They will give you some idea of what to look out for. Then there are extra notes you can read afterwards to check if you missed any of the details.

Hints and Clues

3 The letter might not make much sense now but, who knows, it could be useful later.

6-7 A caped stranger? Will he reappear?

8-9 Some things in the hallway could be worth remembering. Listen out for that clock. It could strike again . . . but what hour?

10-11 Are you seeing double in the bedroom? Surely it's not long since the clock last struck? Have you noticed how loud it is?

12-13 Are they all bonkers? That's a lot of money one of them has tucked in a pocket.

14-15 Is it really midnight? Have you looked at the book and the mirror?

16-17 These dates and times might be useful. Keep your eyes open for familiar faces.

18-19 Is there another early riser in the house? The villagers seem concerned about time.

20-21 What could Lord Midnight want to save so much? Did you read his last words carefully? Did you notice the time?

22-23 Have you recognized anything in the book? Cyanozine: a name to remember . . .

24-25 So it was Lord Midnight who rang Smug. Is there an eavesdropper about? Frank has doubts about the evidence. Take a good look at the happy family group watching Smug leave.

26-27 A secret room – but where? Could Ant be right to feel niggled? How well the caped stranger seems to know the lake.

28-29 Did you spot the newer brickwork? Have you looked at the window next to it? Did you notice the falling gargoyle?

30-31 The portrait could be worth studying. The radio message has some good advice.

32-33 Spin the Potty has quite an audience.

34-35 There seems plenty of useful and useless information here. Can you sort it out? Watch out for clues to the Stone.

36-37 Is the housekeeper alone in the corridor?

38-39 A mystery woodcutter and a branch that just misses them . . . remember the radio warning. Do you recognize the writing?

40-41 A musician may help you find the key.

42-43 How strange, the professor suddenly seems to have no need for his ear trumpet.

By the Way . . .

Did you notice:

. . . the clock strike midnight and the air turn icy cold before ghostly activity?

. . . the ghostly powers of Maurice Midnight getting stronger as the hour of the curse drew nearer?

. . . the evil ghost of the twelfth Lord Midnight appear as Ant and Sally got close to the Stone?

. . . quantum physicist Guy ffoulkes (Sunday Scorcher) has opened a fish shop in Middle-Knight-on-Sea? Whose ghost did he see, do you think?

. . . Hollywood actress Faye Slift and her faithful pooch Clapperboard (Sunday Scorcher) in the train, on the village green and at the cafe?

. . . news of Tuffaware All-Weather Anoraks (Smug's ex-employer, page 34) in the Sunday Scorcher?

. . . the invitation to Polly Tacks' wedding (page 35)? She becomes Councillor Polly Bellowes (Sunday Scorcher).

More about the Midnight Family

Did you work out who everyone was? (If not, reread pages 10, 12 and 16.) Sitting clockwise round the table from Sally on page 12, they are: Posy Tutu, Juster Chuckle, Mervin Midnight, Myrtle and Harvey, Merle, the professor.

You might like to know how Myrtle and Harvey fell foul of the ancient curse. Many years ago as they danced a military waltz at their wedding party, a chandelier crashed down from the ceiling and landed on the nuptial pair as the clock struck midnight. Merle was a more recent victim. Two years ago, she tripped at midnight on the trailing strands of a large cobweb and tumbled downstairs.

In case you wondered about the portraits on page 10: Modesty is married to Juster (she was away on a costume design course from 11-13 November); the man in hiking gear is Milo, who patented the first typewriter to use Mythikan script; John is chief photographer at the Mythikan court and current darling of the society ladies.

Incidentally, the family villa is in Tiktoki, a small village on the Mythikan coast. And did you spot the Mythikan influence in the secret room?
